The Sun, the Moon, and the Silver Baboon
Copyright © 1993 by Susan Field
First published in Great Britain by David Bennett Books Ltd.,
94 Victoria Street, St. Albans, Herts AL1 3TG

For information address HarperCollins Children's Books,
a division of HarperCollins Publishers, 10 East 53rd Street,
New York, NY 10022.

Library of Congress Cataloging-in-Publication Data
Field, Susan, date
  The sun, the moon, and the silver baboon / by Susan Field. —
1st American ed.
      p.   cm.
  Summary: A baboon rescues a star that is caught in a tree, allowing the
night to end and the day to begin, and is rewarded by the sun and moon
with the brilliant colors he wears today.
  ISBN 0-06-022990-X. — ISBN 0-06-022991-8 (lib. bdg.)
  [1. Baboons—Fiction.   2. Night—Fiction.   3. Stars—Fiction.]   I. Title.
PZ7.F476Su   1993   92-44496
[E]—dc20   CIP
                                                                     AC

1 2 3 4 5 6 7 8 9 10
❖
First American Edition, 1993

The Sun, the Moon, and the Silver Baboon

Susan Field

HarperCollins*Publishers*

Every morning the sun rises and scatters golden light across the blue sky.

The rooster crows and the birds sing.
A bright new day begins.

Every evening, when the sun goes to bed,
the sky fills with stars,

and the moon lights the land
with gentle silver moonbeams.

But one night a star came loose from the sky.
Burning bright as a comet, it tumbled to earth
and became tangled in the branches of a tree.

"Please help!" called the moon
to the animals who were awake.
"I cannot leave the sky without all my stars."

"Don't worry," said the owls,
"we will fly up and pull the star from the tree."
"Don't worry," said the insects,
"we will crawl up and eat the branches
holding it."

"We are clever," said the foxes,
"we'll think of something."

But the owls couldn't pull quite hard enough,
the insects couldn't quite eat enough,
and the foxes couldn't think of anything to do.

"Hurry!" said the moon.

"It will soon be dawn."

Sure enough, the rooster soon crowed
and the sun came up.
Now all the animals were awake
and amazed to find the sun, the moon,
and the stars all together in the sky.

"Help me!" the star called to them.
"My tail is caught and I cannot get free."

"Don't worry," said the giraffes,
"we are tall; we will lift you out of the tree."
"Don't worry," said the elephants,
"we are strong; we will shake you out."

"Ha! Ha! Ha!" laughed the hyenas,
who were no help at all.

But the giraffes weren't quite tall enough,
the elephants weren't quite strong enough,
and the hyenas just couldn't stop laughing.

Soon all the animals were talking
and arguing about what to do next.
The noise was tremendous.

The uproar could be heard
even in the distant mountains,
where a brown baboon was sleeping.

His ears began to twitch and his sleepy eyes
slowly opened. He yawned, stretched,
then padded down the mountain
to find out what all the fuss was about.

The animals were all so busy arguing
that they didn't notice the brown baboon.
He took one look at the star in the tree
and saw what needed to be done.

Like a shadow he slipped through
the noisy crowd and climbed the tree.
His quick, nimble fingers loosened
the tangled tail, and soon the star was free.

Up, up, up the star flew, high into the sky.
"Thank you!" said the moon.
"Now the night can end."
And the moon gave the baboon
a coat as silver as moonlight.

"Thank you!" said the sun.
"Now the day can begin."
And the sun gave the baboon
a face as warm as sunlight.

Now the baboon is no longer brown.
From the tip of his new crimson nose
to the end of his fine silver tail,

he shines as bright as any star.